Y0-AAQ-398

# THE DOG BOOK

EDITED BY MARY GOODBODY

Ariel Books

Andrews and McMeel
Kansas City

Frontispiece: *Pointers at Rest*, 1874,
John Charles Dollman

ISBN: 0-8362-4736-1

# CONTENTS

# Introduction

**H**umans and dogs have been inseparable for over ten thousand years. Although some theories claim reindeer or goats were domesticated earlier, most evidence points to dogs as the first domesticated animals. These early descendants of wolves were trained to herd animals and to haul travois (wheel-less vehicles). Later, dogs were used for hunting and guarding. And as humans became more dependent on dogs, dogs became more dependent on humans.

Historically, dog breeders have tried to accentuate herding and tracking skills and lessen aggression—resulting in animals more adaptable than their wolflike ancestors to human ways of life and more vulnerable too. Wolves are pack animals and the hierarchy of the pack is of utmost importance to their survival. Domesticated dogs have transferred their pack loyalty to human groups and have, through the years, come to consider their owners as the *alpha*, or top, dogs. This enables an owner to train a dog and, in turn, to count on his or her unfailing loyalty.

Dogs can breed among themselves without restriction, and while this trait has produced an overpopulation of mongrel (mixed-breed) dogs in our nation's animal shelters, it has also allowed breeders to develop breeds with specific desirable characteristics. Today there are about three hundred purebred breeds of dogs.

Purebred dogs fall into several categories: sporting, working, hound, terrier, herding, and toy. Animals in all these groupings

have evolved from four distinct classifications: dingoes, northern, greyhound, and mastiff. Dingoes are found primarily in Australia but are related to the Pariah dogs of India and the Middle East. The northern group represents dogs that have descended from the gray wolves of northern Europe, such as collies, German shepherds, and huskies. The greyhound classification includes greyhounds, wolfhounds, whippets, and Afghans. Finally, the mastiff group includes Saint Bernards, Great Danes, and bulldogs.

Whether the smallest pugs, the most lumbering Bernese mountain dogs, or the quirkiest garden-variety mutts, dogs have highly developed senses that set them apart from other domestic animals and make them valuable to humans. Most notable are their senses of hearing and smell. Humans respond to sound frequencies of up to twenty thousand vibrations per second, yet dogs respond to those of thirty-five thousand. Dogs' heightened hearing may account for instances when they have sensed earthquakes and avalanches minutes before people have any indication of them.

The olfactory center of the brain is larger in dogs than in humans and by processing large amounts of air through their nasal passages, dogs can smell far more than humans can—some estimates say up to one hundred thousand times more! This heightened sensibility allows bloodhounds to track people even after several days have passed and lets other dogs sniff out illegal drugs hidden in the most ingenious places. And when we take our household pet for her daily walk, she experiences thousands of things through her ears and nose while we humans are relegated to noting only fairly mundane odors and sounds.

The bond between humans and dogs is an ancient one that has only strengthened over time. Today we may rely less on dogs for their inbred talents and more on them for companionship and protection, but we rely on them nonetheless.

# BREEDS: WHO DOES WHAT

ost pet dogs sleep about fourteen hours a day, although they are always ready and eager for a playful romp or a tasty meal. A dozing canine will cheerfully leap from slumber, tail wagging, at the sound of his human companion's approaching footsteps, key in the lock, or car in the driveway. But other dogs go to work every day—and seem to love their jobs!

Humans may first have domesticated dogs to be herders and draft animals, but through the centuries they have discovered an invaluable companion capable of much more. Dogs became vital for hunting, tracking, rescuing, and guarding. It's said that during the eighteenth and nineteenth centuries (and probably earlier) the Tibetan mastiff (a distant cousin to the gentle giant, the mastiff) was regularly left behind in mountain villages to protect women and children while the men traveled as far away as Calcutta to engage in commerce. Russian wolfhounds, direct descendants of ancient greyhounds and closely related to their modern counterparts, were bred to chase wolves—one dog would grab the wolf by the neck and three or four others would pin it down and hold it captive until the hunters arrived to either kill it or take it alive.

These skills are rarely required today, but traits bred into dogs surface as distinct characteristics. Mastiffs and their related breeds still make formidable watchdogs, although most nasty aggression has been bred out of them. Greyhounds and their cousins (known as gazehounds) are as fleet as ever and rely on their keen eyesight when giving chase to rabbits and other animals.

Border collies, currently gaining immense popularity in America, are highly intelligent dogs bred to herd sheep and other farm animals. Their instinctual desire to herd is so strong that even a Border collie raised without exposure to farm animals will, confronting a sheep for the first time, crouch down and stare at the animal with an intense gaze known as a "showing eye," and hold her mouth open in quiet threat.

A retriever who is raised as a happy, suburban family dog will gladly fetch a ball or a stick all day long (given the opportunity). If that dog is taken along on a hunting trip, he will instinctively retrieve the pheasants or grouse—although perhaps not as skillfully as a formally trained retriever.

Giant Newfoundlands, originally bred in the days of clipper ships to rescue sailors who fell overboard, have been known to leap into a swimming pool and drag a frolicking young family member to "safety," mistaking rambunctious fun for real danger.

# The Long and Short of Dogs

The *smallest* dog is the chihuahua. This tiny breed, which many believe originated in ancient Mexico, where it was used as a temple dog by the Aztecs or Incas—weighs no more than six pounds and sometimes as little as two. It stands about five inches tall.

The *heaviest* dogs are mastiffs and Saint Bernards. Mastiffs can weigh as much as 180 pounds, Saint Bernards as much as 170 pounds.

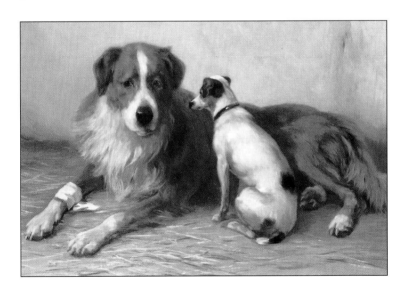

⚞ The *tallest* dog is the Irish wolfhound, which at the most weighs 120 pounds but stands between thirty-two and thirty-four inches at the shoulder. Great Danes, another giant, stand about thirty-two inches at the shoulder and can weigh as much as 150 pounds.

⚞ The *fastest* dog is the greyhound, which can reach speeds of up to 41.7 miles per hour.

⚞ The *hairiest* dogs are komondors and pulis. These breeds originated in Hungary, where the komondor is known as the "king of sheepdogs." Both have dense coats, the outer layer falling in thick cords over a woolly underlayer. Their heavy coats make these dogs practically impervious to any weather.

⚞ The *baldest* dog is the Mexican hairless, which like its close (also mostly hairless) cousin the Chinese crested, originated in Asia, not Mexico. In Mexico, the dogs are often called Chinese dogs. They are not completely hairless but have a tuft of coarse hair on the top of their heads and the end of their tails.

⚞ The *quietest* dog is the basenji, which does not bark but makes a muted yodeling sound when pleased or excited. Perhaps basenjis are the *cleanest* dogs as well. They spend an uncommon amount of time grooming themselves.

⚞ The most *wrinkled* dog is the Shar-Pei, a breed that originated in China and has become extremely popular in the United States. It's not uncommon for the skin to be so wrinkled it covers the dog's eyes, causing problems that often make surgery necessary. When these dogs are puppies, their skin appears far too big for their bodies.

The *oldest* purebred dog is probably the saluki, even though there is evidence the same claim can be made for the Pekingese. Salukis originated in the Middle East as sight, or coursing, hounds that were used to run down gazelles and smaller game. Salukis may have existed as a breed in 2,000 or 3,000 B.C. They are closely related to the greyhound, and dogs resembling both breeds frequently are depicted on ancient pottery from Asia Minor and Egypt.

The *newest* breed (or one of the newest) is the Doberman pinscher. These elegant dogs were bred in the 1890s by Ludwig Dobermann, the keeper of the pound in a small town in Germany, who attempted to breed the finest, most alert guard dog possible. He succeeded. Dobermans are also highly intelligent, and while they can be aggressive they are easily trained, loyal, and loving.

# AMAZING DOG STORIES

Some canine fanciers are convinced dogs possess psychic abilities. How else can we explain the legendary tales of a dog who senses her master's illness or death or one who tracks down his human family after an enforced separation? The following are just a few examples of uncanny canine feats:

A dog once disappeared from the farm where she had lived for many years. Her owners searched for her but after a day or so gave the dog up for lost. Three days later the dog trotted through the open door of a school fifty miles away in search of one of the children in the family who had been sent there to board.

A dog was sleeping in the afternoon sun while his master drove to a nearby town. The guests left behind were startled when the dog leapt from slumber and began howling. After he was calmed down, the dog scuttled into the house and cowered under his master's bed, crying and whimpering. Later, the people involved realized the dog began howling at the precise moment his master was killed in a car accident.

A dog woke his owners by howling in the middle of the night. The couple could not placate the dog, and soon they, too, felt something was not right. Their sons were camping about ten miles away, and the parents drove to the campsite in time to rouse the boys and get them out of the path of a fast-moving fire.

A visitor presented his hosts' Pekingese with a small toy when he left town to go home to a faraway city. Several months passed before the man again found himself in his friends' city. On impulse, he took a taxi to their house without calling first. A good fifteen minutes before his arrival, the Pekingese unearthed the toy from a forgotten corner of the kitchen and raced to the door, eagerly awaiting the visitor—much to the astonishment of his owners and their unexpected guest.

In 1914, an Irish terrier named Prince disappeared from his home in London. Two weeks later he reappeared in Armentières, France, where his master, Private James Brown, was posted. How he had made it across the English Channel and found Private Brown remains a mystery—but his feat has earned him a celebrated place in dog lore.

One of the most famous cases of such tracking involves a collie named Bobbie who was lost in Indiana while his family was on vacation; unfortunately, his family was forced to return home to Oregon without him. Though it was the dead of winter, Bobbie traveled three thousand miles to reach home. His journey was documented and later reconstructed by people who had fed and sheltered the homesick animal along the way.

# THE HOW AND WHY OF DOGS

### Why Is the Dalmatian Called the Fire Dog?

Dalmatians were once fashionably known as "carriage" dogs because they delighted in running alongside horse-drawn carriages or even between the carriage wheels. An excited and exuberant dalmatian running next to a fire wagon racing to a fire was also a common sight—so common they eventually turned into canine mascots in firehouses everywhere.

### Why Is the German Shepherd Called the Police Dog?

These highly intelligent animals were once used as herders and guard dogs and in times of war became trusted couriers. Easy to train, obedient, and strong, they became a favorite of police departments in Europe and the United States. Today they are used to detect bombs and drugs and to locate people trapped in collapsed buildings. Other breeds have joined their ranks, most notably the Labrador retriever.

### Why Do Saint Bernards Carry a Barrel?

Kept by monks high in the Swiss Alps as early as the mid-sixteenth century, Saint Bernards provided companionship and protection. These massive dogs were trained to test snowy passes for safety and came to be relied on for their uncanny ability to predict avalanches and storms. They were also capable of finding travelers trapped by these sudden storms and avalanches, and their loud barks would guide the monks to any travelers in distress. The monks were said to have strapped a small flask of brandy around each dog's neck to sustain the stricken traveler until help arrived.

*How Did the Bloodhound Get Its Name?*

It's not clear how the name came about—except it has nothing to do with this gentle dog's temperament. One theory is that only the gentry (so-called "blue bloods") owned the dogs in old England and so the name evolved. Another theory is that the dogs, who reputedly have the "best noses" (best sense of smell) in dogdom, were used to trail wounded enemies and prisoners by following a trail of blood. Today, bloodhounds, able to follow a trail for miles, are still used for tracking lost children, hikers, and escaped criminals.

# CANINE QUIPS

They went their way, and the dog went after them.
    —TOBIT II:4

The dogs came and licked his sores.
    —LUKE 16:2

Fierce in the woods, gentle in the house.
    —MARTIAL

The dog is devoid of shame.
    —ST. JOHN CHRYSOSTOM

Love me, love my dog. (*Qui me amat, amat et canum meum.*)
    —ST. BERNARD

A barking dog seldom bites.
    —ENGLISH PROVERB

## THE DOG BOOK

Every dog has his day.
—English Proverb

Keep running after a dog, and he
will never bite you.
—François Rabelais

Dogs bark boldly at their own
master's door.
—Edmund Tilney

A good dog deserves a good
bone.
—Ben Jonson

A dog's nose is ever cold.
—John Clarke

If the old dog barks he gives
counsel.
—George Herbert

Hunger and ease is a dog's life.
 —GIOVANNI TORRIANO

The dog teaches thee fidelity.
 —JOHN HORNECK

Histories are more full of
examples of the fidelities of
dogs than of friends.
 —ALEXANDER POPE

Let dogs delight to bark and bite,
For God hath made them so.
 —ISAAC WATTS

He that strikes my dog would
strike me if he durst.
 —JAMES KELLY

Every dog is entitled to one bite.
 —ENGLISH PROVERB

Of all the dogs array'd in fur,
  Hereunder lies the truest cur.
He knew no tricks, he never flatter'd;
Nor those he fawn'd upon bespatter'd.
  —JONATHAN SWIFT

He asks no angel's wing, no
  seraph's fire,
    But thinks, admitted to that
    equal sky,
      His faithful dog shall bear
      him company.
        —ALEXANDER POPE

Bow, wow, wow;
  Whose dog art thou?
  Little Tom Tinker's dog;
Bow, wow, wow.
  —ANONYMOUS

Dogs have not the power of comparing. A dog will take a small piece of meat as readily as a large, when both are before him.
  —SAMUEL JOHNSON

Thy lap-dog, Ruba, is a dainty beast,
  It don't surprise me in the least
To see thee lick so dainty clean a beast.
But that so dainty clean a beast licks thee,
Yes—that surprises me.
  —SAMUEL T. COLERIDGE

A dog starv'd at his master's gate
Predicts the ruin of the state.
  —WILLIAM BLAKE

'Tis sweet to hear the watch-dog's honest bark
  Bay deep-mouth'd welcome as we draw near home;
'Tis sweet to know there is an eye will mark
  Our coming, and look brighter when we come.
  — LORD BYRON

One of the animals which a generous and sociable man would
soonest become is a dog. A dog can have a friend; he has affections
and character, he can enjoy equally the field and the fireside; he
dreams, he caresses, he propitiates; he offends, and is pardoned;
he stands by you in adversity; he is a good fellow.
  —LEIGH HUNT

The dog alone, of all brute animals, has an affection upwards
to man.

   —SAMUEL T. COLERIDGE

The dog may have a spirit, as well as his brutal
  master;
A spirit to live in happiness: for why should he
  be robbed of his existence?
Hath he not a conscience of evil, a glimmer of
  moral sense,
Love and hatred, courage and fear, and visible
  shame and pride?

   —MARTIN F. TUPPER

Old dog Tray's ever faithful,
  Grief cannot drive him away;
He's gentle, he's kind; I'll never, never find
  A better friend than old dog Tray.

   —STEPHEN FOSTER

Every dog is a lion at home.

   —H. G. BOHN

One barking dog sets all the street a-barking.

—H. G. BOHN

The one absolutely unselfish friend that man can have in this selfish world, the one that never deserts him, the one that never proves ungrateful or treacherous, is his dog. . . . He will kiss the hand that has no food to offer; he will lick the wounds and sores that come in encounter with the roughness of the world. . . . When all other friends desert, he remains.

—GEORGE G. VEST

I agree with Agassiz that dogs possess something very like a conscience.

—CHARLES DARWIN

There is no dog so bad but he will wag his tail.

—ITALIAN PROVERB

Newfoundland dogs are good to save children from drowning, but you must have a pond of water handy and a child, or else there will be no profit in boarding a Newfoundland.
—JOSH BILLINGS

To a dog the whole world is a smell.
—ANONYMOUS

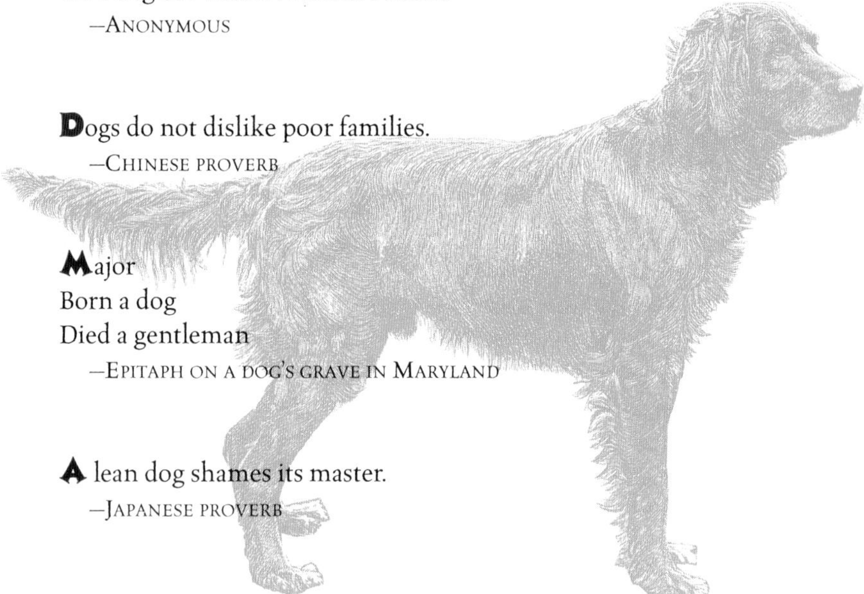

Dogs do not dislike poor families.
—CHINESE PROVERB

Major
Born a dog
Died a gentleman
—EPITAPH ON A DOG'S GRAVE IN MARYLAND

A lean dog shames its master.
—JAPANESE PROVERB

It's funny how dogs and cats know the inside of folks better than other folks do, isn't it?
—ELEANOR H. PORTER

Beware of the silent dog and still water.
—LATIN PROVERB

Our German forefathers had a very kind religion. They believed that, after death, they would meet again all the good dogs that had been their companions in life. I wish I could believe that too.
—OTTO VON BISMARCK

To his dog, every man is Napoleon; hence the constant popularity of dogs.
—ALDOUS HUXLEY

I'd rather have an inch of dog than miles of pedigree.
—DANA BURNET

The dog is the god of frolic.
—HENRY WARD BEECHER

My little old dog:
A heartbeat at my feet.
—EDITH WHARTON

**I** am simply delighted that you have a springer spaniel. That is the perfect final touch to our friendship. Do you know there is always a barrier between me and any man or woman who does not like dogs.

—ELLEN GLASGOW

**W**hy, that dog is practically a Phi Beta Kappa. She can sit up and beg, and she can give her paw—I don't say she will but she can.

—DOROTHY PARKER

**L**ike many other much-loved humans, they believed that they owned their dogs, instead of realizing that their dogs owned them.

—DODIE SMITH

**A** dog teaches a boy fidelity, perseverance, and to turn around three times before lying down.

—ROBERT BENCHLEY

**A**mong God's creatures two, the dog and the guitar, have taken all the sizes and all the shapes, in order not to be separated from the man.

—ANDRÉS SEGOVIA

A dog is the only thing on this earth that loves you more than he loves himself.

—JOSH BILLINGS

Anybody who doesn't know what soap tastes like never washed a dog.

—FRANKLIN P. JONES

Dog. A kind of additional or subsidiary deity designed to catch the overflow and surplus of the world's worship.

—AMBROSE BIERCE

Dogs have more love than integrity. They've been true to us, yes, but they haven't been true to themselves.

—CLARENCE DAY

I loathe people who keep dogs. They are cowards who haven't got the guts to bite people themselves.

—AUGUST STRINDBERG

# NORTH TO ALASKA

"Their tails are high and tongues awag—the twin banners of sled dog contentment."
—CLARA GERMANI


ebate rages over which are the best sled dogs. Some prefer Siberian huskies, the oldest purebred dog in Alaska; others like malamutes, bred by the Eskimos of the same name to be stronger than the husky. Still other sledders find the smaller, faster Alaskan huskies to be superior.

Anyone who has personally witnessed or viewed film of the famed Iditarod race or the newer Yukon Quest International Sled Dog Race can see how much the dogs appear to love their job. As they pull the sleds harnessed to their teammates, they seem to smile with glee, their tongues hanging out. Veteran mushers say getting the dogs to work is no problem; holding them back is the challenge.

The Iditarod is a 1,158-mile race from Anchorage to Nome, Alaska. Equally long and grueling is the Yukon Quest International, which runs from Fairbanks to Whitehorse, a town in the Yukon. In both races, about one-third of the dogs drop out along the way, from either injury, fatigue, or death. Mushers (as the sled drivers are called) cannot stop, leaving their dogs along the way where checkers pick them up and tend to them. This is heartbreaking for both humans and dogs—the dogs, say longtime mushers, hate to miss out on the excitement of the race. It's not uncommon for only five or fewer dogs on a team of the fourteen that started the race to make it to the finish.

During summer, the dogs train by pulling wheeled carts. In August they are shipped to northern Alaska for training on snow and then brought back closer to home for constant training during the rest of the year. The Iditarod takes place the first week in March, the Yukon Quest in February.

# DOG DEVOTION

**R**egardless of breed, dogs are devoted to even the most neglectful owners. Rarely do they turn on the "hand that feeds them." For most people, owning a dog is a purely pleasurable experience. No bad mood, rotten day, or failed business deal spoils your dog's pleasure in seeing you. And his or her unbridled joy can lift your spirits and alleviate stress as nothing else can.

One particularly poignant example of dog devotion concerns a Skye terrier referred to as Greyfriars Bobby. After the burial of his master in a church cemetery, the dog virtually moved into the graveyard. All efforts to relocate him were fruitless. Only his own death fourteen years later separated him from the spot.

It's been documented that simply petting a dog lowers some people's blood pressure, which is especially helpful for those suffering from hypertension. Dogs are frequently used to calm the mentally unstable and cheer up the lonely and aged people confined to rest homes or sanitariums.

One example of a dog's calming presence relates to President John F. Kennedy. During the height of the Cuban Missile Crisis, he reportedly asked for Charlie, the family dog, to be brought into the Oval Office. After about fifteen minutes of stroking the dog's head, he resumed work.

# A Dog Miscellany

More than 36 percent of all American households claim at least one dog: a good proportion of these own two dogs. Veterinarian services for dogs exceed $4.6 billion dollars annually in this country—as opposed to barely $2.4 billion for cats.

Author Rudyard Kipling used to exclaim that his cocker spaniel was his "most sincere admirer."

The black spots on dalmatians aren't there from birth. Dalmatian puppies are born pure white but quickly develop the black splotches that turn into those endearing spots.

Dog fighting was a popular entertainment for certain types of people in early-nineteenth-century Great Britain. Breeders crossed bulldogs with terriers—resulting in tough, hefty, and ferocious dogs that could put up a good fight. Ironically, the Staffordshire bull terrier continued to be bred after dog fighting was outlawed because of its remarkable way with children and general good nature.

During John F. Kennedy's term in the White House, USSR premier Nikita Khrushchev presented the family with a dog, Pushinka. But was she bugged? Would Caroline's little playmate be transmitting top secrets back to the Kremlin? After a thorough inspection, Pushinka was declared to be free of bugs—electronic ones, anyway.

All puppies are blind and deaf at birth. They open their eyes in about two weeks, though it takes another week before they can focus. Hearing, too, takes about two weeks—before that the ear canal is closed.

You may not want to out-stare a dog. Dogs take a stare as a challenge. Should you lose a stare-down, be prepared for the possibility of attack.

President William Howard Taft's Airedale terrier, Laddie Boy, frequently sat in on cabinet meetings—on his own chair. Once the president even threw him a birthday party, inviting other dogs from the neighborhood. The pièce de résistance was a frosted layer cake—made of dog biscuits!

Does your dog prefer you to your significant other? Dogs usually choose one over the other. It may be as simple as who feeds and walks him—or it may be more complicated. One theory has it that dogs prefer the smell of a female over a male; another theory holds that dogs identify with the member of the household with the lowest and most commanding voice—often that of the oldest male. In any case, dogs are often jealous and may find the presence of your partner a threat or at the least a nuisance.

# LIST OF ART CREDITS

Page 6: *Hounds at Full Cry*, n.d., Thomas Blinks
Page 8: *Foxhounds and a Terrier*, 1884, Edward Stuart Douglas
Page 10: *A Good Day's Shooting*, 1883, James Hardy, Jr.
Page 13: *Saint Bernard and Friend*, 1892, Henry Garland
Page 15: *Hamlet*, c. 1870, George Earl
Page 16: *A Domestic Scene*, 1888, William Henry Hamilton Trood
Page 21: *Resting*, 1888, Herman G. Simon
Page 22: *Totteridge Smooth Fox Terriers*, n.d., Maud Earl
Page 23: *Totteridge Smooth Fox Terriers*, n.d., Maud Earl
Page 24: *Prince*, c. 1870, George Earl
Page 27: *Nellie*, c. 1870, George Earl
Page 33: *Luska, A Siberian Sledge Dog in a Snowy Landscape*, c. 1908, Maud Earl
Page 34: *Ch. Merridip Ethel Ann and Ch. Downberry Volunteer*, n.d., Edwin Megargee
Page 38: *English Pointers in the Field*, n.d., Thomas Blinks